In the
Great God's Hair

Also from Westphalia Press
westphaliapress.org

In the
Great God's Hair

Translated from the
Original Manuscript

---

by F. W. Bain

WESTPHALIA PRESS
An Imprint of Policy Studies Organization

Westphalia Press
An imprint of Policy Studies Organization
1527 New Hampshire Ave. NW
Washington, D.C. 20036
info@ipsonet.org

ISBN-13: 978-1-63391-680-7
ISBN-10: 1-63391-680-4

Cover design by Jeffrey Barnes:
jbarnesbook.design

Daniel Gutierrez-Sandoval, Executive Director
PSO and Westphalia Press

Updated material and comments on this edition
can be found at the Westphalia Press website:
www.westphaliapress.org

भंगीभक्तिभावै नमः

IN

THE GREAT GOD'S HAIR

(सुरासुरादिमानदा)

TRANSLATED FROM THE ORIGINAL MANUSCRIPT

BY

F. W. BAIN

पतिः सतीनाम् परमम् हि दैवतम्

Thou art my Lord: I, thy Satī:
I have no other God but Thee.
Motto of the Faithful Hindoo Wife.

James Parker and Co.,

31 BEDFORD-STREET, STRAND, LONDON.

Parker and Son,

27 BROAD-STREET, OXFORD.

1904.

DEDICATED

TO

HUSBANDS AND WIVES.

PREFACE.

----◆----

THE name of the little Indian fable, here presented
to the lover of curiosities in an English dress, is am-
biguous.   We may translate it indifferently, either : *The
new moon in the hair of the God of Gods :* or else : *She
that reduces the pride of Gods, demons, and all the rest
of creation ;* that is, the Goddess of Beauty and Fortune.
To those unfamiliar with the peculiar genius of the
Sanskrit language, it might seem singular, that two such
different ideas should be expressible by the one and the
same word.   But it is just in this power of dexterous
ambiguity that the beauty of that language lies.   As there
are butterflies' and beetles' wings, of which we find it
impossible to say, that they are positively this colour or
that—for according to the light in which we view them
they change and turn, now dusky red, now peacock-blue,
now it may be dark purple or old gold—so a well formed
Sanskrit compound word will subtly shoot and coruscate
with meaning, as do those wondrous wings with colour :
and this studied double, treble, manifold signification of
its words lends to the classic tongue a sort of verbal

sheen, a perpetual undercurrent of indirect suggestion, a by-play of allusion, a prismatic beauty, of which no other language can convey the least idea. For translation must split up what in the original is a unity [a]. And so, our title, according to the value which we choose to assign to its component elements, can be taken to denote, either the hair-jewel of the moon-crested god, or the universal pre-eminence of world-wildering Aphrodite.

And at the risk of incurring the charge of mysticism, I would venture the opinion that our author, in wavering thus between two meanings, two notions at first sight utterly distinct and different, has instinctively seized a subtle analogy, difficult to analyse, and more obvious perhaps in the clear and silent Indian atmosphere than in our own thick and foggy clime: one, however, to which all ancient mythologies bear witness, by invariably connecting their Great Goddesses with the Moon. Night after night, when the fierce fury of the merciless intolerable Indian sun has spent its energy—there are days in the hot weather, when the very last ray from his disappearing rim seems to bore like a red-hot nail into your skull and drain away your life like a great blood leech—when _at last_ the enemy has gone, and the blue mild lustrous

---

[a] And it has often occurred to me that western theologians suffer from want of acquaintance with Sanskrit, for nothing could furnish so apt an illustration of an indecomposable 'trinity in unity' as a compound Sanskrit word.

Dark with its healing, soothing, balmy peace has fallen over the fainting world, I have watched the inexhaustible Beauty of the Moon: and then it is, that there seems as it were to glide into the soul, like a nurse into a sick room, some thing, some presence, vast, infinite, and feminine. The pale and shadowy Holda passes over the dusky dome, with the stars in her violet hair, or is it rather the Blessed Virgin, the ancient hornèd Isis, stretching colossal over the blue, with the Moon beneath her feet? Mere fancy, says the reader: and yet I do not know. Something there seems to be in common, something that all the ancient nations felt, between the beauty of an eastern night with the Moon in its forehead, and the strange consolatory cosmic magnetism that Woman and her mystic Beauty [b] exert over her everlasting patient, Man. Take away her sympathy, and his life would resemble nothing so much as the thirsty earth, parching under an Indian Noon, for ever without a Night.

For the proper comprehension of this story, the English reader ought to know, that just as its keynote—*husband is a good wife's god*—is the very core of Hindoo manners, so the type and model of all devoted wives, the *Sati*, or Constant Wife, *par excellence*, is Párwatí, the wife of the moon-crested God. He and she together are the

---

[b] The πότνια νύξ of Euripides is pure Sanskrit : *patní naktá :* Lady Night.

symbol of wedded harmony, so close and indissoluble,
that they are regarded, under one aspect, as having but
a single body between them, which they share : he is
the god, *whose other, or left half, is his wife:* and poets
compare their relation to that obtaining between a *word*
and its *meaning.*   They are the incarnation of bi-sexual
unity, HERMAPHRODITUS, the ideal type of sacred indissoluble marriage.   In India, marriage is still something
more and deeper than a contract, and has not therefore
yet become ridiculous.   In India, the gods are not yet
pallid spectral ghosts, rationalistic *residua* of neuter gender,
but the immortal lovers of their wives ; and conjugal affection is what it ought to be, typified in heaven, the highest
pleasure even of the gods.   They carry their wives about
in their arms, sit them on their knee, and are inseparable
from them.   And in return, their wives are their devoted
slaves.   *Who,* says the Hindoo proverb, *is the best-loved
woman ?   She that adores her husband as a god.*

CONTENTS.

———◆———

———————————

Note. The legend below the Vignette, representing the Goddess of Beauty, is a beautiful alliterative compound alluding to her origin from the sea. The alliteration evaporates in the process of translation: but the meaning is: *Hail to her whose being is the essence of the tumbling ocean waves, all love, emotion, agitation and broken curves!*

A LOTUS OF THE WORLD.

Prologue.

In the Great God's Hair.

---◆---

PROLOGUE.

INVOCATION.

Adoration to the Four Eightfold Divinities : the Eight Forms of the Lord of Time: the Eight Cardinal Points of Space : the Eight Sections of the Revelation of Panini : and the Eight Pairs of Petals of the Lotus of the World [a].

FAR away, in the quarter of the north, there stands a mighty mountain: of supereminence so transcendent, that even the Mother of the World [b] was willing to call him father: of hue so pure, that even the snowy swans haunting the lake of Mánasa blush in his presence as if ashamed of their own inferiority : of size so gigantic, that the rising and the setting sun throws his shadow on the sky, and

[a] The Lord of Time is Shiwa. Panini's grammar is believed to have been revealed to him by the deity. The Lotus of the world is the goddess of beauty.
[b] Párwatí is the Daughter of Himálaya.

the seven Rishis [c] in their daily revolution turn their
eyes upwards to his peak, glowing like a tongue
of flame at sunset or at dawn.   And there on his
northern face is the home of the Lord of Creatures
animate or inanimate.   There one evening, when
the light of day was flying before the shadows that
rose up pursuing it out of the abysses of the valleys
along the mountain sides, the Daughter of the
Mountain was playing at dice with her lord [d].
And she won from him, first his elephant skin,
and next his rosary of skulls.   And finally she said :
Now, then, I will play thee for that which thou
dost carry on thy head.   And Maheshwara per-
ceived her intention.   But he answered : Very well.
So the Goddess threw the dice, and won.   And
she exclaimed in delight : Ha ! I have won.   Pay
me the stake.   Then Maheshwara gave her his moon.
Thereupon the goddess exclaimed in a rage : Thou
art a deceiver.   Thou dost owe me Ganga, and yet
offer me only thy moon [e].   What do I care for thy

[c] The Great Bear.

[d] As, if we may believe Bhartrihari, they often do, for the lives
of men.

[e] Parwati is represented in Hindoo literature as being very jealous
of Ganga (the river Ganges) because Shiwa caught her, or it, upon
his head.

moon? Then said the god: Why, O fair one, art
thou angry? Is it not this moon which I carry on
my head? But Umá turned away from him in
a pet.

Then the crafty god, who had only teased her
to enjoy the beauty of her anger, preparing to con-
ciliate her, said: Come, the game is over. So now,
give me my moon, which to thee is worse than useless, since thy own face would rob it of its lustre,
being itself a moon always at full. Moreover, I cannot do without it. Then said the goddess: Why
canst thou not do without it? And Maheshwara
said: Know, that were it withdrawn from the forehead of me who am the world [1], this universe would
cease to exist. Then said Umá: How can that be?
And the god said: Of all created things, the new
moon is the fairest. And therefore it is that I wear
it in my hair, as a symbol of that power which is
the pivot of all motion animate and inanimate. For
Beauty is the ruler of the world, and without it,
all would remain plunged in darkness, and motionless. And there is a story connected with this. Then
the goddess, filled with curiosity, exclaimed: Tell
me the story, and I will give thee thy moon, and

---

[1] *Bhawa* means both Shiwa and the world.

forgive thy deceit. And Maheshwara said : Very
well. For this was just what he wished her to do.

Then Umá gave him his moon, and he set it in
his yellow hair. And then he sat down, with his
back against a precipice, and took her on his lap.
And she laid her head on his breast, and prepared
to listen to his tale.

But just as the god was about to begin, he looked
down, and saw, far away on the side of the hill below
him, a man, toiling up painfully over the cold white
snow. And he looked in the middle of that vast
wilderness like an ant, lost among the blocks of
salt in the desert. Then said the god to Umá :
Look! there is a man. What can he be doing
here, where no mortal ever comes ? It were better
to wait and see. Then the goddess exclaimed :
Thou art about to deceive me again. This is
a trick, to cheat me of my story. And Maheshwara
said : Nay, thou shalt certainly hear it without
delay. But first let us discover, what is the object
of this poor mortal. And he called out to the
man : Ho there ! who art thou ? and why art thou
climbing up alone through the ice and snow ?

Then hearing the voice, which echoed like thunder
among the hills, that man fell face downwards upon

the snow. And he said : O Maheshwara, giver of boons, for surely it is thou that I hear and no other, I am come to thee as a suppliant, and all my hope is in thee. Know, that I am a *Kathaka* ᵍ, belonging to the household of the King of Pátaliputra, a city of the plains. And every night before he went to rest, I told him a story, to beguile him and bring sleep to his eyes. So for fourteen years I told him stories, every night one. And then at last, one night, when the time came for him to go to bed, I said to him : O King, my stock is finished, and my fancy exhausted, and now I cannot tell thee any more. Then he looked upon me with red, angry eyes. And he said : O dog, how is this ? Shall I not sleep, by reason of the poverty of thy faculty ? So I fell on my face before him, and said : Let the King show mercy. But I am empty, and the fountain of my invention has run dry. Then he said : Know, that thou art no longer my *Kathaka*, but another has thy place. And know, moreover, that if in three months from to-day, for I will be merciful, and allow thee time, thou dost not tell me a story more curious than anything I have ever heard, I will sever thy empty head from thy body, first

ᵍ A story teller.

tearing out thy useless tongue, and uproot thy
family and all thy relations from the land, like
a furious wind among the trees at the opening of
the rainy season. And immediately he sent and
seized them, and holds them now as hostages for
my return. And so, seeing no other resource, I
have come to thy feet, travelling night and day
without either food or rest. For thou knowest all,
past, present and to come, and now I am in thy
hands.

Then said Maheshwara to his wife : Thou seest,
we did well to wait : and now, this unlucky *Kathaka*
has arrived in the very nick of time. So let him
listen to our tale. But whether for his good or ill,
time alone can show. Then he took the *Kathaka*,
and put him up into his hair. And at the touch of
his hand, that *Kathaka* was delivered in a moment
from all his fatigue and exhaustion, and he sat in the
shadow of that matted hair, illuminated like a forest
of great trees by the diadem of the deity, to overhear
the tale.

And then the god began. And as he spoke, the
Gándharwas, and the Kinnaras, and the Siddhas and
Widyádharas came noiselessly and collected in the
air, and listened with eager ears.

A Lotus of the World.

A Lotus of the World.

I.

LONG ago, in the very beginning, when the world and all its creatures and even the gods themselves were young, there lived in a certain country a King who died, leaving the kingdom to his heir. And this heir was only eighteen years old, and his name was Ranga [a]. And though he resembled in person a combination of the gods of love and war, and was beloved by his subjects, he was generous and hot-tempered and open-hearted and credulous and inexperienced in the ways of the world: and he fell accordingly an easy prey to the schemes of his relations, who plotted against him: and he was ousted from his throne by his maternal uncle, who got the better of him by treachery and drove him out of the kingdom, with nothing left but his life.

---

[a] 'Dye,' 'colour,' and so, 'a field of battle.' (Pronounce to rhyme approximately with *hunger*.)

So Ranga fled, and wandering from place to place in disguise, took refuge in a neighbouring kingdom, having become from the king of a country a wandering Rajpoot, heir to nothing but his sword, and starvation, or dependence on others. And he lost his temper, and flew into a rage with everything in the three worlds. And he cursed, first himself, and next his uncle, and then his relations, and finally even the gods. And he exclaimed : O gods, I cast you all away and disavow you. For all my life I have been pious, and cultivated your divinity, and honoured you with praises and offerings : and yet by way of return, you have paid no attention to me, and allowed me to fall into this condition. Now, therefore, I have become an atheist and a *nástika* [b]. And in his rage he abused the gods, calling them all by their names. And then he said : Henceforth I will worship none of you, and nothing, save only Her who alone deserves adoration, the Great Goddess of Chance and Wealth and Beauty and Fortune, who rules over the three worlds. And he broke out into praises of the goddess, then and there. And he said : O thou who resemblest the sea that produced

[b] An infidel or sceptic : one who ' says no ' or denies.

thee, O Kamalá, O Padmá, O Shrí, O Lakshmí [c], O Beauty of beauties and Lotus of lotuses, show thy miserable worshipper favour. Thou art the very essence and soul of caprice, thou art compounded of the substance of waves and of bubbles and flashes of lightning, rivers that flow and flames that flicker, shifting shadows and woman's wiles. Fair and fickle and false and fleeting, thou dost wander and rove at thy own sweet will from one to another, abiding never anywhere long. Thy only law is thy wanton fancy, thy whim of a moment makes one man rich and another poor, one a king and another a beggar, through no merit of his own or reason of thine. Thou art my only god, for thou only art a true divinity, and I worship the sole of thy foot. O thou feminine incarnation of lustre and grace, white and wayward and tremulous and treacherous as foam of the sea, omnipotent, bewildering, frivolous, inconstant, dissoluble as sand, unsubstantial as dreams, I worship the colour in

[c] The names of the goddess are so innumerable, that if accurately followed they would only puzzle the English reader. They may, however, be tabulated generally as referring either to her *beauty*, her *inconstancy* or her connection with the *lotus*. I have therefore chosen for her name that of *Water-Lily:* the word of all others that best conveys her general attributes to an English ear.

thy long deceitful intoxicating eyes, and the undu-
lating swell of thy wave-like limbs. I offer myself
to thee as a votary and a victim ; do as thou wilt
with me. Raise me or lower me, all is the same
to me, for my devotion is absolute : thou art my
divinity and thy pleasure is my fate.

And as he went on, it so happened, by the decree
of destiny, that WATER-LILY heard him. And without his knowledge, she came near him, to listen to
what he said. And she was much pleased by his
praises, all the more that she was new to them,
having herself but lately risen from the sea. And
she looked at him out of the corner of her long lotus
eyes, and saw that he was very young, and very
handsome ; and she took a sudden fancy to him,
and pitied him. So when he had finished, she cast
at him a glance of approval, smiling with honied
lips like a coquette [d] whose vanity is flattered, and
she said : Come, I will prove to this good-looking
young Rajpoot that he was not deceived, when he
chose my divinity for adoration as more worthy
of worship than that of any other of the gods.

So that very night, to do him a service, she put

[d] Sanskrit is, I think, the only other language that possesses an
exact equivalent for the French.

a strange thought into his head. And Ranga said to himself: Now I have become a worshipper of Fortune, and a gambler, and now I must put her to the proof, and see what she will do for me. For even she can do nothing for those who sit still, and give her no opportunity of taking their part. So he went out and wandered up and down in the streets of the city, looking for anything that chance might throw in his way. And as he passed by the palace of the King, he looked up, and saw at the top of a tower a room with eight round windows, one at each point of the sky. And as he stood looking at it, a man of the town said to him: Rajpoot, what are you about? Do you not know that it is forbidden even to look at the place where the King keeps his biggest pearl. Then Ranga said to himself: I wonder what sort of a pearl that may be, of which it is not permitted even to look at the case. And he went away filled with curiosity; and as he went, WATER-LILY blew it into a flame, till he felt a burning desire to satisfy his wish. And finally he said: I will go this very night, and climb up, somehow or other, and see with my own eyes this wonderful pearl.

So he provided himself with a bow and arrow,

and a very long string, and a coil of rope. And taking all these with him, he went in the middle of the night, and hid himself in the street in the shadow. For the moonlight lit up the palace tower, and buried the other side of the street in the blackness of night. And there he remained, waiting, till he saw the watch come by on its round. Then as soon as it had passed, he came out, and quickly shot the arrow, to which he had tied the end of the string, over the corner of the parapet of the tower. And the arrow fell back to the ground, and Ranga took the string, and tied it to the rope, and drew it up rapidly, till all the string came to an end, and he held in his hands the two ends of the rope. And then very quickly he climbed up with hands and feet like a monkey, and reached the window, and got in through it, leaving the rope hanging down.

II.

AND then he stepped into the room, and started, and stood amazed. For just before him there lay sleeping on a jewelled couch a young woman, looking like a jasmine flower on a bed of its own leaves.

For the moon bathed her in his light, which clung
to her limbs as if it were in love with them : and
she resembled a feminine incarnation of the passion
of love fallen into a swoon of fatigue and pallor
after having conquered the world. And the long
lashes of her shut eyes lay on her cheek like
shadows as far as her mouth, which smiled as she
slept : while the breeze lifted the fringe of the
silk robe that covered her neck, and laid bare the
beauty of her throat, just where it met with the
curve of her bosom, that rose and fell gently as
she breathed. And one hand was under her head,
and the other lay, like an open flower, hanging
over the edge of the bed, from a wrist like a
young reed's stalk.

And as he stood motionless, like a target with
the arrow of Love in his heart, she woke up. For
WATER-LILY entered her dream and showed her
a picture, and said to her : Wake, for I have
brought thee a husband more beautiful than Káma
himself. And when she opened her eyes and
looked : lo ! there he was standing before her.
And instantly she started up, and stood gazing at
him in astonishment. For he answered so exactly
to her dream that she could not believe her eyes,

and doubted whether she had not only dreamed that she woke, and was still really asleep. And then after a while, she said : Art thou a reality, or only a thing in my dream ? And he said : O sleeping beauty, I am a reality : but I wish it were not so : for I would gladly forfeit my life to be only a thing in thy dreams. Then she said : Who in the world art thou, and how in the world hast thou climbed into my room, into which none ever come but my female attendants and the birds of the air ? And he said : O waking beauty, I am Ranga, the King of Awanti, whom his relations have driven from his kingdom. But what do I care : for had it been otherwise, I should never have set eyes upon thee.

But when she heard his name, she started, and could not believe her own ears. And she said : Tell me thy name over again. Then he did so. And she said : Surely I must still be dreaming. Or art thou really sent by the deity ? Tell me thy story from the beginning. And so he did. And she watched him as he spoke, with eyes that she could not take off him. For WATER-LILY bewildered her with his beauty, and poured infatuation into his voice.

And when he had finished, she said to him : O
thou son of a King, beyond a doubt the deity must
have brought thee, for there is in this matter a
thing wholly unknown to thee, so strange, that it
cannot have come about of itself. But now, listen,
for I have a proposal to make to thee. Know,
that the King my father wishes to give me as
a bride to a neighbouring King for the sake of
a political alliance. And rather than be a bride
of that King, I had intended to cast myself down
from this window into the street, for I cannot endure
the sight of him even in a picture. And now thou
hast appeared, as if on purpose, to provide me with
a means of escape. Thou art poor and without
a kingdom, which it may be thou wilt never regain. But thou art my equal in *caste*, and unless
the Creator has made thy exterior a lie, my equal
also in spirit and soul. Wilt thou have me for
a wife, as I am willing to choose thee for a husband,
and carry me down by the rope by which thou
didst bring thyself up ? For I will choose thee
for my husband, of my own free will [e], and share

[e] This is the old *swayamwara*, a recognised privilege of kings'
daughters. The reader must not look at it with English eyes. An
unceremonious marriage is a constant feature in old Hindoo tales:
and it is none the less a marriage.

all thy poverty and evil fortune, and make it
a blessing to thee. Swear to me only that thou
wilt deal with me loyally and share with me, as
with thy other self, all thy troubles and all thy
joys, in this world and the next, and I will place
myself as a deposit in thy hands. And it may be
that I will change all thy evil fortune to good :
and if not, I will help thee to endure it with
patience. And now, say : is the bargain to thy
mind ? And think ere thou givest an answer : for
I will not be bought by thee with anything less
than thy soul.

And when she had spoken, she looked straight
at him, with beautiful eyes, in which there was
neither frivolity nor fear. And Ranga looked back
at her, and his heart swelled in his breast : for
she touched it not only by her beauty but by the
strength of her soul. And he laughed for joy,
and said : Hear me, ye guardians of the quarters
of heaven ! O thou fair woman, thy loveliness is
wonderful, and yet it is the least part of thy excellence. Now thou art worthy of one better than
I am. And yet, if thou wilt give thyself to me
for a wife, I will be thy lord and thy protector in
this life and the next, and thou shalt be my divinity

in human form. And I will want food and cloth-
ing, before thou shalt want sweetmeats and jewels.
And he stooped down and touched her feet, and put
his hand on his head : and then stood and looked
at her with a smile. And she looked at him with
affection, and said : Thou art the man whom I
have desired to have for a husband, and now I see
that my dream was a true one. And now I am
thy wife, and thy servant.

Then he said : Dear wife, now we must go down,
and that quickly, before we are discovered. And
yet, though thou art light as a bamboo leaf, this is
a dangerous thing. Hast thou the courage to make
the attempt? Then she said : What is there to
fear ? For if we fall, we fall together, and meet
death at the same instant. But have no fear: for
I will cling to thy neck with my arms. Then
Ranga laughed. And he said : Nay, I will not
risk my pearl on the strength of thy soft and
slender arms. Then he took from the bed a silk
cover, and twisted it into a rope. And he bound
it tightly round her waist, and then tied it firmly
to his own. And then he drew her to the window,
and looked down. And at that moment he saw
the watch, going its round a second time. So

when it had passed, he said: Now is our opportunity. But she said: Wait: let me bring with
me all the wealth that I have, for at present thou
art poor. And she made a bundle of clothes, and
put into it all her jewels: and flung it down into
the street. And then he said: Art thou afraid?
And she said: I am afraid, but only for thee.
Then he said: Shut thy eyes, and clasp me round
the neck, and hold. So she did. And then Ranga
wove the rope round his legs, and grasped it in
his hands with a grip like that of death, and let
himself slowly down into the street. So he carried
her down to the ground, while the sweat stood in
great drops upon his brow.

And when they touched the earth, she said: Thou
art as strong as thou art brave, and the deity has
sent me a man. But Ranga clasped her in his arms,
and kissed her. And he said: Now I may kiss
thee, for we have faced death together, and I have
made thee my own. But here we must not stay
even for a moment. And he picked up the bundle,
and went away quickly, carrying her in his arms,
and counting the whole world as a straw. And he
said to her: Where shall we go, for in the city
they would discover thee? Then she said: Close

to this city there is another, which is empty and deserted, and inhabited only by parrots and monkeys. Let us go there, and afterwards consider what is to be done. And I will show thee the way.

So he carried her away to that empty city, never once setting her down, for the joy he had in holding her in his arms. And when at last they reached it, he stopped before a courtyard, and went in, and saw in it a deserted cow-house, full of hay and straw. And he put her down, and untied the knots, and set her free. And then he said: Alas! that I should take thee from a palace, to bring thee to such a ruined shed as this. And she said: Where the husband is, there is the heaven of the wife. And he said again: Alas! I am an exile and a wanderer, and I have taken thee from thy relations and thy home. And she said: Is not the wife the child of her husband, and the husband the father and mother of his wife? And what home does she need who has taken refuge in the heart of her lord[1]? Then he put his left arm round her, and took her left hand in his right, and kissed it. And he said: What is thy name? And she

[1] So, in the *Katha Sarit Ságara*, speaks Rupashikhá.

said : I am called Wanawallarí [g]. Then he said : Thou art well named, and now I will be the tree of thy life. Come, and I will find thee a room in this abandoned palace, that shall serve thee for a bridal chamber, and I will make thee a nuptial couch, of hay and straw. For this is our wedding night, and see, yonder is the polar star [h].

III.

BUT in the meanwhile, the gods [i] were aware of what had occurred. For they had heard the abuse that Ranga showered upon them in his despair. And when they saw that by the assistance of WATER-LILY he had obtained Wanawallarí for his wife, they were very angry both with the goddess and with him. And they met in Indra's hall, to discuss the matter and determine what was to be done. But I was not there, for I bore no grudge against Ranga,

[g] 'Wood-creeper:' 'forest-flower.' (Pronounce *wan-* as *nun*, and *-wall-* as *dull.*)

[h] The Pole Star is the symbol of marriage, and the emblem of a bride.

[i] When the gods are spoken of collectively they are generally understood not to include the great gods, Brahma, Wishnu and Shiwa, each of whom has a claim to be considered the greatest.

knowing his ˙youth and the provocation which had occasioned his outburst, and forgiving it. And Nárayana[j] also was absent, for so far from being angry with Ranga, he was pleased with him for heaping praises on his wife, who is a part of himself, as thou art of me[k]. So having met, they said indignantly to one another: This alone would be scandalous and intolerable, that a mortal should insolently load us with abuse for not being at his beck and call as if we were nothing but the slaves of our worshippers. But worse than all, here has WATER-LILY actually rewarded the rascal, by giving him the most beautiful woman in the three worlds for a wife: so that instead of being punished for his bad behaviour, he has actually received a prize. And if this continues, we are wholly undone, and the established constitution of the universe will be destroyed. For it all depends on praise, worship and sacrifice[1]: but if men get our favours without these, who will be at the pains of propitiating us at all? Thus though

[j] Wishnu, of whom Water-Lily is the wife.

[k] Maheshwara is speaking to his wife.

[1] Plato's idea, that the relation between gods and men is one of commercial reciprocity (ἐμπορική) is precisely that of the Hindoos, who lay it down in a hundred places as the essence of the *stithi*, or established constitution of things.

the conduct of this mortal is bad, that of WATER-LILY is infinitely worse. For she has taken the part of a mortal, siding against the gods, merely because she was caught by the cunning fellow's flattery.

Then WATER-LILY laughed, looking at them all askance out of the corner of her long eyes that reached nearly to her ears. And she said : Surely I have done little worthy of blame, if I have rewarded my worshipper for his praises, as all you ought long ago to have done before. For if we pay no attention to them, these mortals will leave us and laugh at us, and then we shall perish for want of our proper sustenance. And so it is not I, but rather you yourselves, that are to blame for leaving him alone. Moreover, after all, he is quite right in considering my power and divinity as stronger than all others, for so in fact it is.

But hearing her words, the gods were enraged, and exclaimed : Fie! fie! And they determined to show her that she was mistaken, and punish her protégé : and they arranged that Indra should descend to the earth, and find him, and make an example of him. But that crafty WATER-LILY said to herself : Now will I show all these foolish gods, and especially Indra, that beauty and fortune are enemies hard even for gods to overcome. And she played the hypocrite, and said to them, with an illusive smile on her beautiful lips : When a fault has been committed, it is for the guilty person to make reparation. Let Indra go down : but I will myself help to bring the sinner to justice and undo my own mischief, by causing the King to discover the whereabouts of Ranga and his wife.

Then the gods were pleased, for she threw them all off their guard by her apparent submission. And they said : She is very young, and moreover, she is a woman, and doubtless she was caught by this rascal's beauty of person, and his flattery : but now she has changed her mind, which is variable as the sea out of which she arose. So we must not be angry with her.

IV.

AND in the morning, those two lovers rose from their bed of hay and straw, which had been to them by the favour of the goddess a nuptial couch sweeter than *amrita* and softer than the down of royal swans. And then, by the instigation of the goddess, Wana-wallarí said to her husband : Dear husband, though we can sleep, we cannot live upon hay and straw, and now thou wilt have to leave me for a little. And she gave him a bracelet, made of rubies as large as pigeons' eggs, and said : Take this, and sell it in the city, and with the money buy provisions for us : and bring back with thee a *wind* [m], and above all, come back as quickly as possible, for I cannot bear thee to be out of my sight. But there will be no danger, for no one saw thee carry me off. And meanwhile I will wait for thee in this empty palace, with my eyes fixed on the road by which thou art to return.

Then Ranga said : I am adverse to leaving thee, even for an instant. And yet, unless we could become cows and eat hay, I must find food for thee, and I cannot take thee with me : so there is no help for it. And he took the bracelet and went away quickly, saying to her : I will be with thee almost before I have gone away.

And as soon as he was gone, Wanawallarí said to herself : Now will I adorn myself like a city to welcome the return of its sovran lord after a long absence. And she chose from her bundle the best of all that it contained, and braided her hair very carefully, bathing in a pool in the court, and using

[m] A species of lute.

its water for a mirror. And when she had finished, she was pleased with her own appearance; and she said to herself : He shall rejoice when he sees me again, and I will watch the pleasure on his face. And yet she did not know, that WATER-LILY was prompting her to adorn herself, to fascinate not her husband, but somebody else. So when she was dressed, she went out and sat in the shade of a great banyan tree that grew over a well near the pool, and fixed her eyes on the path by which Ranga was to appear.

And at that moment, just when, by the contrivance of the crafty WATER-LILY, Ranga was away, and Wanawallarí was sitting under the tree, alone and adorned, Indra descended to the earth, and came along the road, in the disguise of an old Brahman, towards the empty palace, in which he knew that those lovers had passed the night. And Wana-wallarí looked and saw him. And saying to herself : This is only an old Brahman, and I have nothing to fear : she sat still by the well, watching him approach. So the disguised Indra drew near her. And when he came up, he looked at her, as she sat still under the tree. And he was thunderstruck, as if by one of his own bolts, by her beauty, not knowing that

WATER-LILY was pouring into it her own fascination to bewilder him, and employing as an instrument the charms of Wanawallarí. For her lovely limbs were half revealed and half concealed by the folds of her robe of silver muslin, as the moonlit mist that rises from the spray at Gangotri both hides and shows the rocks over which the water flows : and she had bare feet and heavy golden anklets, and great gold bangles that made her little hands look smaller, and jewelled armlets that encircled her arms just above the elbow, making those round arms seem even rounder than before: and a string of great pearls round her neck, and one great grass-green [n] emerald in her jet-black hair. And as he looked at her, the clearness of his mind was disturbed and agitated by emotion ; for she struck him hard, as she looked at him with calm eyes. And he said to himself : Why, this mortal woman would laugh at every Apsaras in my court : and if WATER-LILY has seen her, I cannot understand how she has not died of envy. And he said to Wanawallarí : O lady of the lovely eyes, thou art surely the wife of Ranga, whom I have come to see ?

[n] This epithet (*shashpashyáma*) would appear to mean that *shadowy* hue which is seen in the hollows of *grass* when lit by the sun,

Then Wanawallarí said : Sir, it is true that I am his wife, though I cannot tell how it could be known to thee so soon. For yesterday I was no wife, but an unhappy maiden, and last night was my wedding night. Then said Indra : O fragile one, all things can be known, by the power of asceticism and years. And it is not hard to see that thou art the bride of a day. For thy lotus eyes are full of new happiness, and peaceful, and not, like those of an unmarried maiden, agitated and alarmed.

Then said Wanawallarí : Brahman, if thou art come to see my husband, know, that he is away : and I am awaiting his return. And it does not become a woman of good family to talk to strange men. I pray thee, therefore, to leave me and come back again another time. Then said Indra : Moon-faced lady, old age is a condition hard to bear, and full of evils, and it would be altogether unendurable, but for its privileges : of which one is, that an old man may converse without scandal even with the young wife of another man. For when the fire is extinct, what has the fuel to fear ? And to judge by thy appearance, I am old enough to be thy father, were thy years even double what they are. Since, therefore, I have been so highly

favoured by fortune ° as to find thee instead of thy
husband, let me seize my opportunity, and ask
thee in his absence, what evil spirit prompted thee
to choose for thy husband one known to be a scorner
of the gods, and therefore likely to feel their vengeance, and come to a sudden and disgraceful end.
For they rarely prosper, whom the gods have determined to punish. Therefore, would it not be thy
better course to repent while there is time, and
this opportunity is afforded thee by his absence,
and leave him to his fate, and save thyself, and
sever thy connection with a man doomed and in
danger alike from the gods above, and the father
from whom he has stolen thee below?

V.

And as Wanawallarí listened to his words, she
discerned instinctively danger to her husband from
that old Brahman. And she said to herself: Who is
this that knows all about us already? Is he a spy of
my father's, who knows me by sight? Or can he
be some god in disguise, come down to injure my

° As in fact, he had been, but otherwise than as he thought.

husband, or corrupt me for my beauty? For such things have often happened before. And she looked at him coldly, and said: Brahman, thou art an evil counsellor; and I should indeed be more worthless than stubble, should I abandon my husband, for whom I have only just abandoned my parents. Nor can I imagine, by what means all should be known to thee, unless thou art a god. But wert thou the very god whom, if thou speakest the truth, my husband has offended, I would tell thee, that my husband did well to scorn one who practises the very thing that he condemns in my husband, in seeking to seduce the wife of another from her religion. Dost thou not know that to a true wife her husband is a god? And if it were the case, as thou sayest, that my husband had abandoned his gods, would it make the case any better, if I should forsake him who is mine?

Then said Indra: O lady, luckless and lovelorn, art thou, alas! already so far corrupted by associating with a scorner of the gods, as to side with him against them? Know, that he shares the guilt of a crime who approves of the criminal when it is done: and thou dost as it were thyself offer insult to the deity by defending its offender.

Then said Wanawallarí : I know no deity but my husband, and follow him without question or reason, as night follows day. And so far from being wrong, this is the duty of a woman, for it is *dharma* [p], established from the very beginning, and having its roots in her nature and his. For once there was a time, when there were neither men nor women, but the universe existed alone. And then one day, when the Creator was meditating with a view to further creation, he said to himself : Something is wanting to complete this Creation which I have created. It is blind, and unconscious of its own curious beauty and excellence. Thereupon he created a man. And instantly the Creation became an object of wonder and beauty, being reflected like a picture in the mirror of the mind of the man. Then the man roamed alone in the world, wondering at the flowers and the trees and the animals, and at last he came to a pool. And he looked in, and saw himself. Then full of astonishment, he exclaimed : This is the most beautiful creature of all. And he hunted incessantly through the whole world to find it, not knowing that he was looking for himself. But when

[p] *Dharma* means law, duty, custom and religion combined.

he found that in spite of all his endeavours he could never do more than see it on the surface of pools, he became sad, and ceased to care about anything. Then the Creator, perceiving it, said to himself: Ha! this is a difficulty which I never foresaw, arising naturally from the beauty of my work. But now, what is to be done? For here is this man, whom I made to be a mirror for my world, snared in the mirror of his own beauty. So I must somehow or other cure this evil. But I cannot make another man, for then there would be two centres to the circle of the universe. Neither can I add anything to the circumference of Nature, for it is perfect in itself. There is necessary, therefore, some third thing: not real, for then it would disturb the balance of the universe; nor unreal, for then it would be nothing: but poised on the border between reality and non-entity. So he collected the reflections on the surface of the pools, and made of them a woman. But she, as soon as she was made, began to cry. And she said: Alas! alas! I am, and I am not. Then said the Creator: Thou foolish intermediate creature, thou art a non-entity, only when thou standest alone. But when thou art united to the man, thou art real in participation with his substance.

And thus, O Brahman, apart from her husband a woman is a non-entity and a shadow without a substance: being nothing but the mirror of himself, reflected on the mirror of illusion.

VI.

THEN said Indra: O slender-waisted lady, thou arguest well of the general duty of wives; and yet this does not vindicate thy own infatuation in consorting with such a one as is he whom thou hast chosen for thy husband. Thou hast sacrificed the flower of thy virgin beauty on an altar unworthy of it, and fallen from the state of a queen to be the wife of a wandering vagabond.

Then said Wanawallarí: O Brahman, every flower, sooner or later, must fade, for this is its destined and inevitable end. Fade it must at last, whether it be on the head of a queen in the palace, or alone in the depths of the wood. And who shall say, whether it is not better for the flower to wither in the wood, than as an ornament in the hair of queens? So then, if I have abandoned my royal position, and betaken myself to the forest and solitude with my husband, what is lost that deserves to be regretted? Art thou so sure in my case that it is a loss and not rather a gain, if like a flower I live and fade in the forest alone? For once there was a king who was betrayed by his wife. And he cast off his kingdom like a snake its old skin, and threw away everything like a blade of grass, and turned his back upon the world. And he went, not to the Ganges, but away into the great southern forest, for he said : Let me go where I shall never again see a human face, or hear a human voice again. So day after day he went on into the unknown depths of that terrible forest, till after a time he found himself alone with his shadow among the giant trees. And then, all of a sudden, those trees came abruptly to an end. And he looked and lo! he stood on the bank of a great river, whose water was studded as far as his eye could see with a countless host of lotus flowers that coloured that region blue. And every lotus had for its lover a great golden bee, that buzzed about it like an incarnation of the sun, come down to earth after self-multiplication, like Krishna among the *Gopis*, in order that each lotus might think itself alone beloved. And the king marvelled at the sight of that lonely lotus haunted, bee-booming river, and he lived there till he died, alone. And if the Creator could frame those fair flowers in the midst of that wilderness to live and die with never an eye to see, surely they were better than if they had all been gathered to fade upon the hair of a million queens. Moreover, where my husband is, there is no solitude: for all the company that I need is his.

VII.

THEN said Indra: O dark-haired lady, thou talkest of thy husband as if thou hadst known him from thy birth ; whereas thou didst set eyes on him for the very first time in thy life, last night. And how then canst thou tell that he will not cease to satisfy thy soul, or that he on his part may not weary of thee, and cast thee carelessly away : for ye are strangers that have met by chance.

Then said Wanawallarí : Brahman, thou art speaking only to beguile me : or else thou art but a poor pundit on the essence of the world. Know, that a woman recognises in an instant, with unerring sagacity, if only she be fortunate enough to see him, the man proper to be her husband: for this depends not upon the shallow and casual experiences of this life, but the store of reminiscences of a former birth. Moreover, there are instants and atoms of time containing in themselves causes and consequences that run both ways into the two eternities of the past and the future, being as it were the fruit of the one and the seed of the other: and many times it happens that the twinkling of an eye determines the destiny of a soul. And this was my case: for since I saw my husband, I am other than I was, altered for infinity by a moment of illumination and the nectar of mutual recognition. Has not the Creator planted in the core of all things animate and inanimate aversions and attractions to be their destiny, not to be controlled or disobeyed? As once there was a mournful maiden, married against her will to a certain king. So when they were united, horror and the hatred of life entered and inhabited her soul. And every time that he approached her, she fell into a swoon that resembled a foretaste of death. Then finding it impossible to come near her, that king was amazed. And he said to himself: Surely there must be for this extraordinary antipathy some extraordinary cause, buried in the mysterious darkness of the past. For other women, so far from shunning my embraces, welcome, and even court them, becoming *abhisárikás* [q] for my sake: for I am a very handsome man. And he went and offered sacrifice in the temple of Maheshwara. And standing before the image, he exclaimed: O thou knower of past, present, and future, if thou dost not reveal to me the cause of this aversion, I will this very moment cut off my own head. Then the image of the deity uttered a loud laugh. And it said: O foolish king, this is a very simple thing. Know, that long ago, in a former birth, thou and she fell by reason of sins previously committed into the bodies of brutes. And she became a snake, and thou a peacock. Hence she cannot endure even thy proximity, for thou dost retain a strain of the nature of the peacock, and its vanity. And the king said: But why, then, do I feel no corresponding aversion for her? And the god said: Because in another birth thou wast a bird of the race of Garuda, of which snakes are the appropriate food. Moreover, women retain

[q] An *abhisáriká* is a woman who goes of her own accord to her lover, or, as we might say, throws herself at his head.

traces of these affections and abhorrences more permanently than men, because emotion is of the essence of their soul : and plunged in bodies, like vats, they carry away, like pure water, the stain of the dye. So learning the truth, the king took another wife, and lived with her in peace. And thus, O Brahman, I was drawn to my husband the very moment that I saw him by a cord woven in a former birth, irresistible and invisible as the power that draws grass to the amber jewel. And now I have been rivetted to him by our marriage as with adamantine bolts.

VIII.

THEN said Indra : O lady of large eyes and heavy lashes, thou arguest like a partisan in thy own favour : yet is thy action only the result of sudden passion, which made thee forget thy maiden modesty, and like an *abhisáriká* hasten to thy husband's arms, moving not like a woman of good family, but by self-will and independence, attracted by the beauty of thy husband.

Then said Wanawallarí : O Brahman, in this

I have done nothing unbecoming a maiden of my *caste*. For the daughters of kings have had from the beginning the privilege of choosing their own husbands. But they show their family in this, that when once they have chosen, they abide by their decision, and cling to their husband with a grasp that laughs at the endeavours of even death to break its hold. And if I have done wrong in yielding to the fascination of my husband, I will make amends for it hereafter. And yet the fault is rather that of the Creator than my own. Wouldst thou blame the lotus for intoxicating bees? Or why did the Creator give beauty to women or to men, but to snare each other's souls? And even the gods come under thy reproof, for which of them is not subdued by the beauty of his wife? Nay, there are some who have even gone astray, bewildered by the infatuation of beauty in a sex other than their own [r]. Why dost thou blame me for obeying the nature of a woman, and worshipping that masculine beauty which is my goal? For the three worlds are only an incarnation of action such as mine, and thy accusation would rob this universe

[r] This, though she knew it not, was a home-thrust : for of Indra, as of Zeus, there is a scandalous chronicle.

of motion and life, which subsist only by virtue of reciprocal attraction. For beauty dazzles and allures, and being itself only an illusion draws every creature after it, like a cunning piper, into that vain revolving dance which sages call the world ; and which without its object would vanish like a dream when the dreamer is awake. And we all move in an everlasting round, like the drops of water in a waterfall, leaving an impression of permanence upon the eye of the observer ; yet is this permanence only an illusion, and due to the perpetual flow of its fleeting and fantastic atoms. And in our momentary life, one thing only is essential, to taste if we can a single drop of the nectar of true love, which is possible, for every atom, only if it can catch a glimpse of that peculiar beauty which is the proper object of its soul. And therefore, O Brahman, I am not ashamed of adoring the beauty of my husband, but I glory and rejoice in it, like one who has found the fruit of her birth. And like a moth, I flew into his candle, and became a willing victim. And I am ready to endure all the consequences of my choice. And when I waver in my allegiance to my lord, I will acknowledge the justice of thy reproof.

IX.

THEN said Indra: O low-voiced lady, when did a woman's tongue ever lack excuses for her behaviour with her lover? and thy ingenuity is not inferior to that of any of thy sex. And yet, say what thou wilt, thou knowest that thy father will not share thy own opinion in this matter: and thou and thy husband are likely to come to a speedy and miserable end, as soon as he discovers where you are.

Then said Wanawallarí : Brahman, thou art partly in the right, for it is possible that sudden anger may cause my father to act rashly. And yet even here, time may show that thou art mistaken, for policy is the first consideration with my father, and he may see reason to forgive us. But let him do as he pleases, he cannot harm me. For whether he lets my husband live, or kill him, he cannot now divide us, nor deprive me of my right to follow him alive or dead, for a wife belongs not to her father but to her husband. So if we live, we live, and if we die, we die together. And death is no evil, but only an inevitable change: and often for the better, if the life to which it puts an end be one of works deserving a reward. For once there were two kings of the desert, called Haya and Gaja [s]: and they were deadly enemies. And Gaja set upon Haya, and killed his son and captured his wives and his capital and drove him away. So being reduced to extremity, Haya entered the service of Gaja, who did not know him by sight, as a personal retainer. And while he waited for an opportunity to revenge himself, Gaja was attacked and his army destroyed by a third king, and he fled into the desert, badly wounded, with only Haya for his companion, hoping to cross over the desert and get back to his own capital and be safe. So they two went together over the desert. And having but one skin of water, they could give none to their horses, which died : and they went on on foot.

Then Gaja said to Haya : There is hardly water in this skin to carry one man across the desert ; much less two : and now our fate is sure. And they went on, and day by day the water shrank. And Haya carried the skin. And one night, as Gaja slept upon the sand, Haya remained awake. And he looked at the skin of water, and said :

[s] 'Horse' and 'elephant.' (Pronounce Gaj- to rhyme with *trudge.*)

One man could cross the desert on this water, but not two. And now my enemy lies there before me. So he sat in silence, with his naked sword in his hand, alone in the desert with the twinkling stars, watching Gaja as he slept, all night long. And in the morning they went on. And as the sun grew hotter, Gaja grew fainter, for he was weakened by his wound. And he said to Haya : Let us drink, even if we die. So they drank. But Haya put shut lips to the water, and took none into his mouth. And so they went on day by day, and Gaja drank the water. But Haya only put it to his mouth, and looked at it with glittering eyes, and lips closed like the door of death.

And at last there came a day, when Gaja said : My wound has robbed me of my strength, and now I can go no further. Moreover, the water is done. Then Haya said : Be strong : it is but one day more. But Gaja said : Go thou on and save thyself, and leave me here to die. And he fell upon the sand, and lay in a half-swoon.

And then Haya stooped, and took him in his arms, and staggered on. And as he went, he grew giddy, and his senses wandered, and the desert danced before his eyes. And he heard in his ears the plash of water, and the drums of the desert rang in his head, and behind him the spirits of the region of death called to one another across the sand, and laughed and mocked him as he went like one going in a dream. So he struggled on in the loneliness, while his life ebbed away, withering like a flower in the burning fire of that angry sun. And suddenly he heard in his dream the voice of Gaja, crying above his head : Lo ! yonder is the city away before us, and now we are saved. Then Haya set him down. And he said : O King, I am Haya, and now I have brought thee over the dusty death. And he fell with his face upon the sand, and went to the other world. But Yama saw that action and remembered it : and Haya rose in the next birth out of mortality and became a spirit of the air.

X.

THEN said Indra : O lady, whose bow-arched eyebrow is touched with the exquisite beauty of faint surprise, certainly that brave Rajpoot deserved his reward : but what is there in common between his action and that of thyself and thy husband ?

Then said Wanawallarí : Brahman, that which is common to us is our reward. For I regard my meeting with my husband as a special favour of the deity greater even than the rise of Haya in the scale of being, and due beyond a doubt, like that, to some meritorious action in a previous birth. But as to our actions in this life, there is still time : and I will endeavour to efface whatever there may be of egotism and independence in this action of mine by the whole tenor of my future obedience. And do not therefore be too apt to estimate the future of our lives by the past : for while life itself endures, there is the possibility of change, and many times it has happened that the very close of life has brought with it something contradictory of its whole previous course. As once there was a dog without an owner. And it had nowhere to go, and nothing to eat : but it scraped for itself a miserable subsistence from the refuse of chance, eating and drinking out of gutters : and it was very thin, and covered with sores and wounds : for everyone that saw it cursed it and abused it and drove it about, beating it with sticks and pelting it with stones ; so that living in terror of perpetual death, it carried its tail between its legs, and in its sad eyes hunger fought for the mastery with fear and shame. So it continued to live, until at last its end was near. And one day when it was so weak that it could hardly walk, there came by it along the road a bullock cart, containing a number of women who were coming from a wedding feast. And seeing the dog, they all began to jeer at it. But one of those women got down from the cart, and going up to the dog with compassion in her heart offered it a piece of cake. And the dog looked at her with wistful eyes, not understanding; for in its whole life no one had ever done it a kindness of any sort. And after a while, it wagged, very gently, the very end of its thin tail. And thus, O Brahman, none can tell with certainty the end of a life from its beginning: and it may be that my husband, or even I myself, may find opportunity to redeem ourselves from thy censure hereafter, by conduct deserving of thy approval.

XI.

THEN said Indra: O ripe red fruit lipped lady, for all that thou canst say, thou canst not persuade me that thou hast not done very ill in forsaking thy father's house for the arms of this stranger. Wilt thou find reasons to prove that it is the duty of all kings' daughters to run away with robbers that break into their palaces by night?

Then said Wanawallarí: O Brahman, my case is an exception and not a rule, for all rules have exceptions. Moreover, though maybe thou wilt disbelieve it, know, that even I would not have acted as I did, but for just this husband and no other. For though I may appear to have acted in this matter with indiscretion and frivolity, yet it has been not in accordance with my nature, but against it; and therefore it furnishes no rules, either for any other person, or even for myself. For once in a way a coward may be brave, and a miser generous, and a wise man foolish, or even a sane man mad: and so may a woman give herself away without reserve to that one man who wakens the sleeping adoration in her heart, and lights in her soul the everlasting fire, without forfeiting her claim to be enrolled among the 'pure women of the world. And this I know to be my case, for my conscience is at ease, and does not blame me. And she who has her own soul on her side requires no other witness to her purity. As once there was a king with many wives, who were all unfaithful and untrue to him, but one. So having to go upon a warlike expedition, he gave each of them a lotus, and said : Keep this red lotus, and show it to me when I come again ; and its colour shall be a proof of thy fidelity. For I received it from the deity, and it will never wither, so long as thou art true to me alone. And then he went away. And as soon as he was gone, all those wives with one exception amused themselves with other men. And very soon they all looked to see their lotuses, and found them withered away and dead. And they all became afraid, being conscious of their guilt, except the one. Then presently news arrived that the king was coming back. And when he arrived, all his wives appeared to meet him, rejoicing and adorned, with protestations of affection. And the king said : Show me all your lotuses. And they showed them, each her own : and lo ! they were all fresh and red as when he gave them.

Only that one good wife gave him a withered lotus,
And she said: O my lord, I know not how it is,
that all these lotuses are fresh. For here is my
lotus dead and withered, contrary to thy word:
and yet my heart has never thought of any man
but thee. Then all those other wives exclaimed
against her, for they hated her: and they said: O
king, she is corrupt, and we all know it: and now
here is the proof. But the king looked at them,
and he laughed. And he said: O ye fools, how
could a lotus remain fresh for so many months?
Now are you all condemned by your own endeavours to conceal your guilt. But she alone was
acquitted by her heart, and did not fear the withering of her lotus: and she alone is pure, and worthy
to be my queen. For the lotus that did not wither
was the lotus of her heart.

XII.

THEN said Indra: O lady with a smile like the
opening of a *bakula*[t] blossom, even if thou wert

[t] *Mimusops Elengi:* a very fragrant flower celebrated in Hindoo
stories, *Bakuli* being a favourite name for a princess or heroine.

thyself deserving of excuse for falling victim to
the innocence and tenderness of thy own maiden
and unsophisticated heart, yet canst thou not ex-
culpate thy husband, for coming like a thief at
night and stealing thee away. Well didst thou
say thyself, that like a moth thou hast flown into
the fire, and burned away thy gauzy wings.

Then said Wanawallarí : Brahman, how can a
weak woman hope to avoid a fate that overtakes
even the greatest gods ? Was not the god of love
himself shrivelled like a butterfly in the fire of
the Great God's eye ? And how then could I escape
from the fire in the eyes of him who is to me in
place of God ? Come now, shall I prove to thee
that my husband has done no harm but rather
good ? Dost thou not know that women are like
leaves, and love is like the wind, that blows hither
and thither among the trees at its own sweet wayward will. And to every tree it comes and shakes
the leaves. And some fall on the instant, while
others remain fixed for a little time upon the bough :
but sooner or later all are doomed to fall, save only
those which unkind fate keeps unnaturally fastened
to wither and decay upon the tree. For whether
they fall or do not fall, they cannot escape the

common inevitable end. So what is gained by the
leaf that remains upon the tree? Were it not
best to yield and fall, when wooed by a breeze
loaded with the fragrance of sandal from the mount
of Malaya, than wait to be torn, willy-nilly, from
the bough by an overbearing ungentlemanly blast?
Now show me if thou canst a man more worthy
to be my own or any other woman's husband than
is he who stole me from my tree: for I have seen
innumerable men as I looked from my window,
and never any one to be compared with him. For
he is strong and I am weak: and he is brave and
I am timid: and a king was his father, and so
is mine: and he is beautiful, and I can read in all
men's eyes as well as thine that I am too. For
beauty shakes the heart of whosoever sees it,
whether man or woman, and uproots it, and if it
is very powerful snaps like cotton threads all the
fibres that fixed it to its ancient soil, and carries it
away, as his did mine. And so the heart of
a woman is blown about and carried along by her
husband, wherever he may choose to take her.
And they who would have it otherwise are not
pundits in the mystery of life. For my heart lay
buried in utter darkness, like the earth at night:

and there came in my husband at the window, like the sun at dawn : and in a moment I was full of the red delight of love. And now my soul is his by right, for all that now it is, is due to him : and its colour and its gladness are only the reflection and the consequence of him. Take him away, and all would disappear? And wilt thou blame the sun, for turning black night to rosy dawn?

XIII.

THEN said Indra : O lady, whose body diffuses all around it the camphor perfume of high *caste*, thy pleading for thy culprit husband and thyself resembles the reflection of a peacock's tail in silent water : for it is various and beautiful, and yet it is nothing but illusion ; for thou art bewildered and intoxicated with the glamour of first love, which lends eloquence to thy tongue and makes thee take a wandering Rajpoot for a god.

Then said Wanawallarí : O Brahman, all is illusion in this world, and yet some illusions last longer than others : there is no other distinction or dif-

ference between them.   And what does it matter
even if, as thou sayest, my faith in my husband
were illusion, provided only that it lasts, at least as
long as life?   What can be more illusive than a
dream, yet who can discern the illusion of a dream,
till by its coming to an end he wakes?   Is not illusion as good as reality, until it is discovered to be
illusion?   Thy words are therefore naught, until my
illusion is destroyed.   Yet this may never be, for
time may be wanting to detect it.   It is a gain, even
if it endure only for to-day, for who knows for certain
that he will see the rising of another sun?   As once
there was a king, who was playing at midday in the
season of hot weather in the water with his queen.
And standing in that cool and crystal water, first
he made her into statues, while he watched the
pictures of her attitudes reflected in its mirror:
and afterwards he splashed her with the water, till
the queen began to look like a young moon peeping
through the clouds: for her wet clothes clung to
her body, showing the outline of her limbs, and her
dark blue hair was loosened from its braid and fell
round her in a mass, and rained into the water.   And
when they were tired, they rested together in the
shade of the ruin of an arbour that stood by the

pool; and the king fell suddenly asleep with his head on her lap. And he dreamed that he went hunting in the morning, and as he went, he saw a Brahman lying asleep under a tree. And when at evening he came back, there was the Brahman still asleep. So he sent his attendants to awake him. Then after a while they returned, and said : Mahárájá, this Brahman will not wake, do what we may : and yet he is not dead, for he is warm, and breathes. Then the king had him brought into the palace, and laid upon a bed. And there that sleeper lay for seven years, while the king lived his life. And at last, one day, that Brahman suddenly awoke. And he looked round in amazement, and exclaimed : What is this ? for only just now I lay down to sleep beneath a tree. And the king said : Brahman, thou hast lain there asleep for seven years, and all the while I have done my daily duties, and made wars and peaces, and begotten sons and daughters, who have grown whilst thou didst sleep upon the bed. And just as the Brahman was about to answer, the king suddenly awoke himself. And he heard the voice of his queen, saying : *Aryaputra*, art thou asleep ? Then the king said : How long have I slept ? And

she said : Thou hast only just laid thy head upon
my lap.   Then the king looked at her with astonishment.   And suddenly he exclaimed : Ha ! all
is illusion, and all is momentary : what is time and
what is a dream ?   I have slept for seven years : and
there are thy wet clothes still clinging to the twins,
that, like arrogant rebels, stand out from thy breast.
And beyond a doubt, thou and I are but dreaming,
and presently we shall awake.   Kiss me quickly,
without losing a moment, while yet there is time.
And she thought he was mad.   But she bent obedi-
ently towards him, with the *bimbá* [u] of her lower
lip pursed for a kiss.   And at that very moment,
the roof of that ruined arbour fell in and crushed
them, and they died on the spot : awaking from
their dream before they had time to kiss each other,
as the king had feared.   And who can tell, O Brahman, whether it may not be our lot also, to wake
from the dream of our life, before there is time to
wake from the illusion of our love ?

[u] A fruit employed by Hindoo poets as we speak of 'cherry'
lips.

XIV.

THEN said Indra : O lady of limbs that are shaped like serpents sweeping and winding in curving coils, thy words are prophetic, and thy own dream is likely to prove but a short one, with a bitter awakening even in this life. What if this husband of thine should have left thee already, never to return ?

Then Wanawallarí said with a smile : O Brahman, hast thou never seen a man of the *caste* of fishermen, fishing for little fishes in the water of Ganges ? Once they have swallowed the bait, they cannot escape, being held fast by the cord. And then being caught, they are roasted by their captor at the flame of a fire, and devoured. Dost thou not know that the God of love has a fish for the sign on his banner ? And why, save that he is himself a fisherman, who fishes for the hearts of men, using women for his bait ? And so only last night he fished for my husband, and caught him, using me for his lure, and now the fish can no longer escape. For he has swallowed the bait, and the cord of no fisherman was ever so strong as that by which my husband

is held by that Master Fisher, Love. For such is
the cunning of that god, that so far from shunning the fire at which he cooks them, his fishy
victims bask and rejoice in it : and the longer my
husband has been away from me, the more and
more certain his return, and the more intolerable
to himself his absence. For now he resembles one
frozen with the ice and snow of the Himálaya
mountain, and very soon he will utterly perish,
unless he comes back to warm his cold heart at the
flame which Love keeps ever burning in my own.
For know, that the heart of a loyal wife is the altar
of Love, on which the sacred household fire ever
burns. And it shines out in the darkness, to guide
the travelling husband home : and in his absence, its
pure beam on the black night resembles the streak
made by gold on the dark touchstone of fidelity.
And no fire goes out while there is still fuel to feed
it : and mine is not yet utterly exhausted. Nor
was I so foolish as to let my husband leave me,
without a security for his return. For know, O
Brahman, that of all the Creator's creatures, there
are only two that do not require to hunt for their
legitimate prey, but wait quietly while it rushes to
destruction in their toils of its own accord. And

of these, one is a spider[x], and the other is a woman.

XV.

THEN said Indra: O thou delicious lady, Love has cast his spell upon thee, or as thou sayest, caught thee on his hook ; and now thou art like one who looks from afar upon the desert, and admires its delusive beauty, not knowing, by reason of inexperience, what its nature really is. And doubtless thou art right, and thy husband will hold thee fast, while the blossom of thy beauty is fresh and fragrant with morning dew ; but when thou art worn and dusty in the heat of the day, beware ! lest he should throw thee away. Thou dost not know what lies before the vagabond's wife.

Then said Wanawallarí : Brahman, she that chooses her own husband resembles a bold gambler, that stakes his all upon a single cast of the die. And if she has chosen lightly, guided only by frivolity and the desire of selfish pleasure, evil and woe will

---

[x] This word might also mean a fisherman, a 'netmaker.'

be her doom. But if she has made her choice not
obeying her own inebriation but rather spell-bound
and appropriated by the master spirit of her true
husband and the fatal moment [y] that brought her
like a planet within his grasp, then poor is her
nature and feeble her devotion if she be not prepared
to follow him blindfold, and take all that fate in
his form may involve in her lot For she that
leaves all behind her and comes at the call of her
husband does so not out of pleasure, though the
pleasure is supreme, but as it were against her own
will, and simply because she cannot help it, because
he is he. And thereafter nothing can befall her,
for the fruit of her birth is obtained. For it is better
for a woman to find her master, even if he should
afterwards ill-use or desert her, than never to discover
him at all. For every woman needs a lord, but many
never find him. But when she has found him, let
him treat her how he will, she is his. But if she
finds the wrong man, though he may treat her as
a queen and adore her as a goddess, yet she never

[y] The Sanskrit word *lagna,* meaning an astrological moment of
planetary conjunction, has become, in modern Maráthí, the common
term for a *marriage.* It is, I believe, essential for a Hindoo marriage
that the horoscopes of the bride and groom should correspond.

will love him and her heart will not be happy, because she is not his, and he cannot command her.
For an elephant is held by a chain, and a woman
by her heart; and the essence of her love is the
sense of obedience; for no woman ever loves any
man, unless she knows that he is her master to be
obeyed without a murmur whether she will or no.
Yet in this is no slavery, for she loves her chain,
and likes to be dominated by the man she adores.
And for every woman, happiness is misery, with
the man who is not her true master : but misery
is happiness with the husband who is. And no
one but a woman can understand the indescribable
pleasure of willing obedience to her lord ; for it
arises from the peculiarity of her nature which man
does not share ; for his nature is not to obey but
command. And now, my husband is my lord, and
I am his slave. And if he continue to love me,
it is well : and if not, still it is well, for he cannot
prevent me from worshipping him. For though the
Creator may if he pleases drive away the swan from
the lotus-haunted pool that he loves, he cannot with
all his omnipotence deprive him of his desire of
the pool. Nor can any destiny overpower the loyalty
of a wife : for she whose devotion to her husband is

diminished by circumstance or change was never his wife, but a stranger, joined to him by accident and error and called by a name that was never hers.

XVI.

THEN said Indra : O lady of swelling bosom and lofty soul, though thy husband has found in thee a jewel through no merit of his own, still thou canst not deny that he is a scorner of the gods, and therefore doomed to bring himself and thee also into disaster arising from their anger.

Then Wanawallarí rose up and stood before him. And she crossed her hands over her bosom, and lowered her long dark lashes over her eyes. And she said : Brahman, now I am a wife, and it may be shall soon be a mother, and many things I know now that yesterday were unknown to me. And now, let me ask thee a question. If I should have a son, and if, when he grew to be a man, in a moment of forgetfulness and anger due to evil fortune he should curse me as the author of his misery : tell me, what would be my duty ? Should I abandon and forsake him ; or should I not rather forgive and condone his offence, considering it rather as the outcome of a moment of passion than the deliberate act of a hardened ill-doer?

And she raised her lashes, and looked at him with clear irrefutable eyes that penetrated his soul, and waited for him to reply. And Indra was abashed before her, and could not meet her glance. And he struck his hands together, and exclaimed: O woman and wife, subtle-witted and silver-tongued, whose incomparable beauty is rendered irresistible by the soft love-light in thy young bride's eyes, I am conquered by thee, and thy husband is blest in thee: and well is it said, that a virtuous woman is higher than the gods. Know, that I came to punish thy husband, but thou hast redeemed him, and stood between him and the wrath of heaven. Take thy husband and lead him into the good path, which is thy own, and save him, if thou canst, from thy father's vengeance, as now from mine.

And instantly he vanished from before her eyes, and flew up into the sky. And WATER-LILY saw him go: and she looked after him with triumph in her almond eyes, and laughter on her vermilion lips. But Wanawallarí started, when she saw that illusive Brahman disappear. And she drew her breath, and stood, like a startled fawn, with wondering eyes and moving breast, while the colour came and went upon her cheek. And then she said to herself: It was as I thought, and that old Brahman was some deity, descending in a mortal form to try me. For his eyelids never moved [1], and his body cast no shadow, and he knew all that had occurred to us as no mortal could have known it. But now, let me remember his words, and stand, if I can, between my husband and my father's anger. And as she spoke, she looked, and saw her husband coming quickly towards her along the street.

XVII.

AND then with a cry of joy, she ran towards him, while the colour leaped into her face. And he came towards her very quickly, and said: See, here is food, and wine, and a cup out of which we will drink together, and a lute for thee to play. But O! how beautiful thou art; and I am faint

[1] A peculiarity of gods, denoted by fixed epithets: as *animisha, stabdha-lochana,* one *'whose eyes are fixed,' 'who does not wink.'*

and hungry, but only for the nectar of thy arms and thy lips. And she put her arms round him, and they stood together for an instant, while their souls met rapturously after separation, hovering in agitation at the door [a] of their thirsty lips. And then, after a while, she said : Come, thou art here, and thou art hungry, and so am I. Let us eat first, and then it may be, thou shalt kiss me again. But Ranga put his burden down, and took her in his arms. And he kissed her, till her lips turned pale, as if for fear lest her breath should abandon her. And then they sat together by the well, and eat and drank, kissing each other between every mouthful, and smiling with tears in their eyes, utterly forgetting their own names.

Then when they had finished eating, they got up and wandered about in each other's arms, like a human symbol of myself [b] and thee, watching the parrots screaming in the fig trees, and the monkeys climbing over the roofs of the deserted houses, and sighing by reason of excess of happiness, and laughing without a cause, while the day passed away like a flash of lightning, and the sun went

[a] *Dantachada:* precisely the Homeric ἕρκος ὀδόντων.
[b] Maheshwara *loquitur*.

to his rest in the mountain of his setting, and the
moon rose. And then Wanawallarí said : Come
let us go back, and find the wine, and we will
have a drinking bout : thou shalt drink for both
of us, and I will sing and play to thee on the
lute, and dance with my shadow to attend me,
to show thee my accomplishments [c] and give thee
pleasure in the light of the moon. So they did.
And Ranga sat under the tree, with the cup of
red wine in his hand, while she danced [d] and
played and sang to him, looking in the moonlight
like a feminine incarnation of the camphor-essence
and beauty of the moon come down to earth to
entrance his soul and wean it from all care for
earthly things. And he watched her with intoxicated eyes, and said to himself : Surely she is a
portion of the celestial delight of heaven that has
somehow assumed the form of a woman ; or a piece
of sky-crystal tumbled by accident to earth, laughing in its purity at the grossness of the materials
by which she is surrounded !

[c] There is a pun here : she compares herself to a digit of the moon.
[d] Dancing is associated by the modern Hindoos with lax morality :
but this cannot always have been the case, for in most Hindoo
romances the heroine is accomplished in that art.

So they two delighted each other in that ruined city, bathed in the moonlight, and the ecstasy of the mutual infatuation of first love. But in the meanwhile, the jeweller, to whom Ranga had taken Wanawallarí's bracelet, was filled with amazement when he saw it. And he said to himself: Where did this Rajpoot get such a jewel, which could not be matched in the city? So after buying it for a very low price, he followed Ranga without his knowledge, and saw him making purchases in the bazaar: and finally he dogged his footsteps at a distance, when he returned to the empty city. And when those lovers met, that curious jeweller looked round the corner of the street, and saw them. But they never noticed him, for they were lost in oblivion of everything in the world except themselves. Then still more astonished than before, the jeweller said to himself: The beauty of this woman exceeds that of all others as much as does that bracelet, which is doubtless hers, all other jewels of its kind : and now there must be a story in this matter. So after waiting a while, and watching them, he returned slowly and reluctantly to his own house. And when he got there he found the whole city in uproar. And when he enquired the reason,

the people said : Somebody or other has come by
night and 'carried away the King's daughter. And
there is a great reward for the man who can find
out who took her, and where she is.

And instantly the jeweller took his bracelet, and
ran at full speed to the King's palace. And being
admitted, he told his story and showed the bracelet.
And the King recognised it as his daughter's ; and
sent, without a moment's delay, guards, who led
by the jeweller, went as quickly as possible to the
empty city. And while those lovers, forgetful of
everything, were intoxicating each other's eyes in
the moonlight, suddenly they heard a shout, and
the King's guards rushed in and seized them, and
carried them away prisoners to the King.

But WATER-LILY saw them go. And she tossed
her pretty head, and yawned. And she said : Now
I have kept my promise to the gods, and caused
the King to discover the hiding - place of these
foolish lovers. And I have done enough for this
fellow, and I am beginning to be tired of him.
Strange ! how soon these mortals pall on me ! they
have nothing permanently interesting about them,
and any fancy that I have for them passes off like
a shadow almost as soon as it arrives. But still,

he is the best looking man that I ever saw. And so, I will do him one more good turn, and then leave him to shift for himself.

XVIII.

So Wanawallarí and her lover were carried quickly back to the palace, and brought in by the guards before the King. And when the King saw them, he clapped his hands : and he said : Ha ! so the flown bird and her decoy are caged. And now, what shall be done to the daughter who brings disgrace upon her family by running away with strolling Rajpoots ? Or what does the thief deserve who breaks into the palaces of kings by night and carries off their daughters and their choicest gems ?

Then said Wanawallarí : O father, let not anger blind thee to justice. For though I have acted independently, I have done nothing, as thou shalt find, to disgrace either myself or thee. For know, that this husband of mine is, like myself, the child of a king, and even himself a king. And as for me, did not Draupadí and Damayantí choose their own husbands ? And was not Shakuntalá wedded

to Dushyanta by the Gándharwa ceremony, and
Bharata was their son? But the King said:
Enough! O daughter! Thy husband shall die with
the rising of the sun, however it may be with thee.
Then said Wanawallarí: Then wilt thou be the
murderer of thy own flesh and blood: for he is
my husband, and Í will die with him. And the
King laughed. And he said: O my daughter,
that art no longer my daughter, dost thou really
think to persuade me that I am obliged to this
Rajpoot for carrying thee away; or to thee, for
causing scandal by running away with him, like
an independent woman of no family, of thy own
accord?

Then said Wanawallarí: O father, listen for
a moment: and afterwards put us both, if thou
wilt, to death, and not him alone. This is no
common matter, and sure I am, that the deity has
a hand in it. Tell me only this, for thou knowest
me well: was I one to act lightly? And the King
said with bitterness: It is that very thing which
makes thy behaviour incomprehensible. For I
thought thee another Sitá: and lo! thou hast
leaped from thy window into the arms of a wandering Rajpoot! Who can fathom the nature of

women or the bottomless abyss of their frivolity?
They talk to one man, and look at another, and
think of a third e. They are but deceit incarnate
in a form of illusion. For four things are insati-
able of four : ocean, of rivers, and death, of mortals,
and fire, of fuel, and woman, of man.

Then said Wanawallarí: But one question I have
to ask thee, and it is the last : Of whom didst thou
destine me to be the bride: Was it not the King
of Awantí? And the King said: Yes. Then
Wanawallarí took her husband by the hand. And
she said: Here he is. And now I am his wife :
and be sure, that the deity himself has brought
this about. For know, that last night, this man
climbed into my room. And I paused for a
moment ere I gave him to the guards, for I pitied
him for his beauty and his youth. And I said to
him: Who art thou? And he said : I am the
King of Awantí. And I started, and I listened
to his story ; and as I listened, he stole away my
heart through my eyes and my ears. And I saw
before me, not that hideous Rákshasa for whom
I was destined as a victim of thy political necessity,

e This is the ungallant opinion of Bhartrihari, based it may be on
some fierce fiery pang of a jealous heart, long since gone to dust and
ashes.

but the God of Love in human form. And know, that rather than become the bride of that other, who has driven away my husband, and keeps by force a kingdom not his own, I would have thrown myself down from my window, and I looked upon myself as already dead. For I knew, that policy was thy first consideration, and that I must be a sacrifice. And I looked upon him who is my husband, as I listened to his tale, as one sent by the deity himself, and as new life in the form of a man. For how could chance have brought into my window the very king to whom I was betrothed, if not by the express agency of the deity himself? Moreover, thy own interest was concerned: and if thou wilt let thy reason speak, I have done thee no injury, but a service. For why wouldst thou have had me the bride of that usurper, but to ally to thee the kingdom which he holds? And how art thou injured, if thou hast gained for the husband of thy daughter not the false king but the true? Do my husband right, and instead of putting him to death, help him to regain his throne: and thou shalt gain for a bad ally a good one: as I have gained for myself a good husband for a bad one: and a kingdom for all three of us.

Then the King exclaimed in amazement: This is but an idle tale, concocted between thy lover and thyself to deceive me. And then Ranga spoke. And he said: O King, till now I have not spoken, for I would not beg my life, and I considered it as a thing gone past recall. But know, that as to what concerns myself, thy daughter has told thee nothing but the truth : and so far from arranging it together, she never told me anything about it, and all that concerns my uncle, and thyself, and her, is news to me, and I hear it for the first time. So now put me, if thou wilt, to death, or if thou wilt, keep me under guard, and make enquiry. And if it is not true, put me to a hundred deaths instead of one. Or lend me, if thou wilt, but a little force, and I will put myself upon my throne. For my subjects love me, and submit to my uncle only from necessity ; and be sure, that he covets thy alliance only because he knows that he is weak, and cannot stand without support. So do according to thy will. Only visit not thy anger on thy daughter, for I only am to blame. And yet, I think that even I am not without excuse. Look at her as she stands, and blame me if thou canst ; for even a god would fall if tempted by a beauty such as hers. Yet know, that it was accident and not intention that brought about our union. For I climbed up into thy tower, not knowing what was there. And now, I am in thy hands.

And as he spoke, WATER-LILY put beauty in his limbs and courage in his voice. And the King watched him, against his will, with admiration. And he said to himself: He says well, for my daughter might turn a sage from his devotion. And he himself is one, whom a maiden might be forgiven for admiring, for I have never seen a finer man. Certainly, if only the tale were true, he would make a son-in-law well fitted to my daughter. So when Ranga had made an end, the King stood looking at him under his brows, balanced in the swing of irresolution, between his anger, and his affection for his daughter, and the influence of the tale. And as he stood in silence, Wanawallarí came and knelt at his feet. And she said: O father, do not kill him, but protect him, and it will be thy gain. But as for me, deal with me as thou wilt. For I have acted rashly, and I deserve only punishment and disgrace. I am only a weak woman, and his beauty carried me away.

Yet know, that thy posterity is within me, and there stands the father of thy grandson. And dost thou think that such a man as that would beget a son to bring disgrace on thee and me? And she looked at her father, with tears falling from her eyes like rain. And they fell upon his anger, and melted it, and overcame him. And he took her in his arms, and kissed her, stroking her hair with his hand. And he said : Dear daughter, I cannot be thy enemy, even if I would, and the tears in thy eyes have brought tears into my own. And if thou hast acted very rashly, I will not follow thy example. Let thy husband stay with me, and I will investigate the truth : and if it be as thou sayest, we will see what can be done for him.

Then Wanawallarí caught him round the neck with a cry, and wept upon his breast. And by the help of that King, Ranga regained his throne, and got Wanawallarí for his queen. For a husband's fortune is the virtue of his wife.

XIX.

AND then, WATER-LILY left him, and quitted the earth, and flew up to heaven. And there she found all the gods assembled in Indra's hall. And instantly she began to mock them. And she exclaimed: Now you may see how vain it is for any or even all of you together to contend with me. For this Rajpoot has attained prosperity in spite of your dislike, by my favour; and as for Indra, he was utterly worsted by beauty, when he met it in the form of a mortal woman. And after having flouted them, she went away, laughing in triumph as she went, and casting back upon them over her shoulder glances out of the corner of her almond eyes that pierced the heart of the gods like poisoned needles.

And then they looked at each other, and said : We have all been made fools by this wicked WATER-LILY ; and now this is utterly intolerable. And Indra said : Though that mortal scoffer, whom I forgave for the sake of his wife, was to blame, yet she will bring him back to his duty. But the real culprit in this matter is this mischievous goddess. For she took us all in by a show of submission, and has shown favour to a mortal who flattered her vanity, out of a capricious desire to tease and annoy us all. Therefore now we must punish and put a stop to her proceedings : for if she be allowed to go on, everything human and divine will be thrown into confusion. And now she is young, and capable of improvement : but unless she is kept in order, she will get worse and worse. Therefore we must look to it without loss of time.

Thereupon they all came in a body to me [f]. But I said to them : This is not my affair. Go to Náráyana, if you have any complaint to make against WATER-LILY. For to punish the wife is the duty of none but the husband. And I sent them away. Thereupon the gods hunted through the universe for Náráyana, but for a long time in vain. And then at last they found him alone in the very middle of the sea, lying on the leaf of a lotus as it floated about on the waves, sucking his left toe, and buried in meditation. And as they came and ranged themselves in silence before him, the adorable Harí politely took his toe from

[f] sc. Maheshwara.

his mouth, and gazed at them curiously with great dreamy eyes, as much as to say : What do you want of me ?

Then the gods, with Indra for spokesman, having first bowed respectfully before him, said : O Achyuta, we have come to complain to thee of the conduct of thy wife : who has made us all ridiculous by taking the part of a mortal that showered abuse on us, simply because he loaded her alone with flattery and praise. And she laughs in our faces into the bargain, though she is the youngest of us all. And now she has hidden herself somewhere or other and cannot be found. Therefore our prayer to thee is, that she may be taught by thee the due bounds of propriety and decorum, and respect for her elders. For our dignity is diminished by the wilful independence of her behaviour.

And then, that husband of WATER-LILY whispered very gently the name of his wife. And low though it was, the sound of that whisper vibrated through the three worlds into the uttermost parts of space : and the universe echoed to its tone like a lute whose strings tremble at the touch of the wind. And as that ubiquitous murmur sank and died away into a hush, the sea began to bubble and foam, and suddenly the goddess of beauty rose up out of the lather of its waves for the second time [g]. And she stood with her little feet resting on the back of a tortoise, and the sea water dropping from her limbs that seemed to sparkle with the beauty of its salt. And her neck resembled a shell, and on the pearl of its surface was reflected the dark shadow of the green emeralds that hung round it; and she held in one hand a dark blue lotus of exactly the same colour as her long-cornered, lash-netted, shadowy eyes. And the graceful creepers of her soft round arms, and the extremities of her smooth and tapering legs, whose knees bent a little inwards, were loaded with rings of red coral that blushed with envy at the colour of her lips, which smiled as if conscious of their own superiority : while her bosom, whose two breasts were turned slightly away from each other like sisters that have quarrelled, rose very gently up and down as if keeping time to the music of the sea. And she held up with her left hand a coil of the blue hair which fell in masses from her head, and encircled her like a cloud blown by the breeze:

[g] The first time was when she was born, at the churning of ocean.

and its end trailed away over the ocean waves. So she stood in silence, bending a little forward, till a three-fold wrinkle showed in the soft fold of her slender waist, while the foam plashed and lapped over the back of the tortoise that supported her, hungry to kiss the arched instep of her tiny pearly-toed feet. And her eyes looked far away, fixed on the horizon of that sky-bounded ocean plain.

And the gods looked at her in silence, and then at each other. And each knew what the other thought, though no one spoke. And each one said to himself: How is it possible to accuse such a beautiful creature as this of anything whatever, much less punish her. So they all stood gazing at her, confounded and abashed, and intoxicated, and silent, while she waited before them, and Wishnu watched both her and them with dreaming eyes. And suddenly the gods turned, as if by mutual consent. And without speaking, they all flew away together over the sea, and disappeared on its edge like a flock of birds.

And then Wishnu looked at his wife with a glance of ineffable affection. And after a while he beckoned to her with a smile. Then WATER-LILY came at once, and sat down at the feet of her lord, and began to rub them gently with a hand softer than the lotus which she laid beside them. And Wishnu watched her, opening and closing his dreamy eyes, while the waves rocked their lotus couch quietly up and down. And the sun set, and the night fell, leaving them alone together in the darkness on the bosom of the sea.

Epilogue.

Epilogue.

---◆---

AND then, Maheshwara ceased. And he put up his hand, and took the *Kathaka* out of his hair, and set him down. And he said : Thou hast heard : Go now, and tell thy story to the King.

But instead of going, the *Kathaka* fell with his face upon the snow. And he exclaimed : O Maheshwara, O Shambu, O Three-eyed Trident-bearer, O Lord of All and Giver of Boons, thou hast sanctified my ears with the nectar of thy tale. Yet O ! grant me yet one other boon. So Maheshwara said : What is that ? And the *Kathaka* said : O show me but a single glimpse of that wave-born beauty, as she rose out of the sea before the gods.

Then the Great God said privately to his wife : See now, how these dim-sighted stupid mortals ask for they know not what, and rush ignorantly upon their own destruction. And he said to the *Kathaka* : Dost thou really desire to see that immortal beauty? The _Kathaka_ said: Yes. Then said the god to Umá: Go quickly and find WATER-LILY, and tell her only that I have need of her favour for a moment.

Then his wife flew away like a flash of lightning. And they waited there in silence, the Great God and the mortal, while the diadem of the deity shone out over the lonely peaks of snow. And after a while, the Daughter of the Mountain returned, bringing WATER-LILY with her. Then that beautiful one said: I am here: and now, what favour has the Great God to confer upon me?

And Maheshwara said: O darling of Náráyana, here is a poor devil of a mortal, to whom I have granted a boon. Do me this favour: show thyself for a single instant. And he said to the _Kathaka:_ Look up now, and see.

And the _Kathaka_ raised his head, and looked up into the dark expanse of sky, stretching over the pallid snowy moonlit peaks. And suddenly, the goddess was revealed against it, like a picture painted on a wall. And for a single fraction of an atom of an instant of time, there flashed in his eyes the vision of that blinding loveliness, and over two hills of snow a pair of dark blue eyes shot into his own, and withered his heart like a blade of dry grass in a sheet of forest flame. And he uttered a cry, and caught at his heart with both hands, and fell upon the snow dead.

Then said Maheshwara : How could a mortal expect to endure such a beauty as thine ? But this dead body must not remain here. And he took it by the foot with his purifying hand, and flung it away. Then that empty corpse rushed with a whistle through the ice-cold air, and fell like a meteor into the Ganges at Haradwára. But the soul of that unlucky *Kathaka* instantly returned to earth and was born again. And he became a poet, who wandered in the world all his life long, hunting with a heart on fire for the eyes he could never find.

PRINTED BY JAMES PARKER AND CO.,
CROWN YARD, OXFORD.

Featured Titles from Westphalia Press

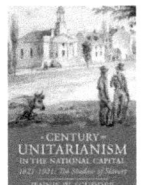

A Century of Unitarianism in the National Capital, 1821-1921
by Jennie W. Scudder

Jennie Scudder's work traces the sometimes controversial history of Unitarianism in the District of Columbia, centering on All Souls Unitarian Church. The account includes the development in the District and surrounding towns in northern Virginia and Southern Maryland.

Boston Unitarianism 1820-1850
by Octavius Brooks Frothingham

From the author, "Many years ago I proposed writing something in memory of Dr. Frothingham, but abandoned the project on account of the meagerness of the biographical material. Within the twelvemonth, a warm friend and admirer of his asked me to prepare a memoir."

The Great Indian Religions
by G. T. Bettany

G. T. (George Thomas) Bettany (1850-1891) was born and educated in England, attending Gonville and Caius College in Cambridge University, studying medicine and the natural sciences. This book is his account of Brahmanism, Hinduism, Buddhism, and Zoroastrianism

The Bahai Movement: A Series of Nineteen Papers
by Charles Mason Remey

Charles Mason Remey (1874-1974) was the son of Admiral George Collier Remey and grew up in Washington DC. He studied to be an architect at Cornell (1893-1896) and the Ecole des Beaux Arts in Paris (1896-1903), where he learned about the Baha'i faith, and quickly adopted it.

The Old Spanish Missions of California
by Paul Elder

This work only portrays a partial and sanitized tale of the Spanish missions in California and their impact. The missions relied on agriculture to fund themselves, and sought to convert and colonize the Native people and their land. Rebellions against the missions occurred since the missionaries sought to destroy native culture.